THE SPIDER & THE DOVES

THE STORY OF THE HIJRA

Farah Morley

In the name of Allah, the One God,
Most Compassionate, Most Merciful

Let me tell you a story– a story that, like all the best stories, is true. Long ago, in the deserts of Arabia, there was a place called **Makkah**. Makkah was a small but beautiful city, full of camels and caravans, colours and perfumes. The desert was a huge, empty space and Makkah was a special place: a place to rest, a place to trade, and a place to pray.

In the desert surrounding Makkah there were rugged mountains, hills and caves, and among those caves there was one named Thawr. Thawr was home to a little spider. Now, it can be very lonely in the desert, for the days seem long and the nights seem longer. The little spider often wished for the company of a friend. Sadly, few animals stopped by its cave, and even those that did, didn't stop for long.

But one day, a pair of young doves flew by. They liked the look of the cave on Mount Thawr and they decided to build their nest there. They gathered twigs, grasses and spider silk, and wove them into the branches of a shrub at the cave's mouth. There they were protected from the wind and sun. It was a perfect place for a pair of nesting doves.

The spider was so happy to have some friends at last! These were no ordinary friends. They were birds that could take wing and bring back stories of all they had seen. Every day the doves would rise high into the sky and fly into the desert to see what they could find. Often, they would fly all the way to Makkah. They would always find grain and crumbs, water, and interesting tales in Makkah.

At the heart of the city was a well, named **Zamzam**. Now a well with cool, refreshing water is an important gathering place in any desert town. But next to this well stood the most important, special place of all: the **Kaaba**, Makkah's sacred heart. This towering, cube-shaped building had been built thousands of years before, by the Prophet **Abraham*** and his son. To this sacred place, people had come, generation after generation as they do today, to make **Pilgrimage**. The pilgrims came to worship God, and find peace and safety. The people of Makkah had a rule that no one must harm any person or creature near the Kaaba – not even an insect.

There were always crowds around the Kaaba, buying and selling things in the market, and sometimes stopping to pray. But after the days of Abraham*, when the people of Makkah had worshipped One God alone, people started to bring other gods with them. They brought idols of wood, stone or clay, and left them there. At the time of the little spider and the doves, there were hundreds of different idols placed around the Kaaba. People could often be seen praying and making offerings to their gods. Few were the people who bowed down to One God alone, and the other worshippers thought them strange!

The doves would sit and watch the people bustling about. They would especially look out for the faces they knew. There was one young man in particular who fed the birds, and the doves learned to recognize him. Muhammad* was his name. Muhammad* was special, like the heart of Makkah, for he was from the family of Abraham*. Like his great ancestor, Muhammad* was a Prophet and Messenger from God.

The Prophet Muhammad* was known for his kindness, honesty and trustworthiness. Never did he pass anyone by without giving them a smile or a helping hand. This may not be odd where you live, but it was an odd thing in Makkah, for many people had forgotten kindness and good manners just as they had forgotten God. But even if you lived in the kindest street in the world with the best mannered neighbours, they would still be no match for Muhammad*. His goodness shone out like a lamp in the darkness. The doves could see his light and were drawn to him. When they returned to their nest in the evenings, they had plenty of tales to tell about this extraordinary man.

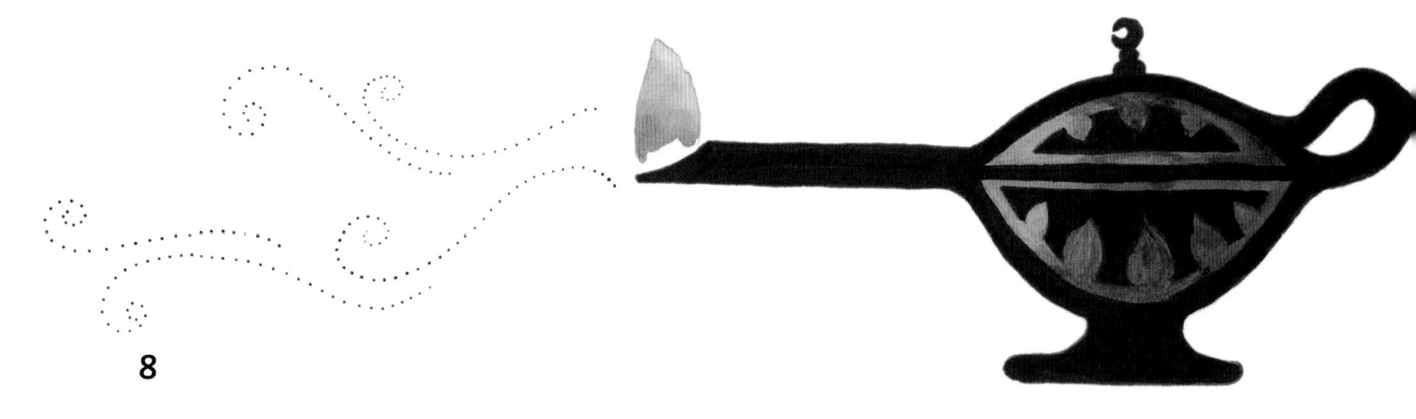

'What does he look like?' asked the spider one day.
'His face is like the moon,' said one dove.
'And he is always smiling,' said the other.
'Yes, and he has a small gap between his front teeth, which are very white,' both doves cooed.

The doves told the spider that when Muhammad* was still a young man, a great flood had damaged the Kaaba. The townspeople had needed to repair it. While rebuilding the walls, the leaders of Makkah had started to argue about which of them was the most important. For only one man – and his tribe – could have the honour of returning the special **Black Stone** of the Kaaba to its place. It was a great honour to touch the Black Stone, and each tribe believed that *it* should have that right.

Their fighting continued, with voices growing louder and hotter, until someone said, 'Let us ask the next person who enters the holy sanctuary to decide.' All agreed. Suddenly, to everyone's joy, they saw Muhammad* approaching.

A great cheer went up. 'It's Muhammad, the Trustworthy one! Let's ask him to decide.'

Muhammad*, who was younger but wiser than many of the greybeards among them, listened carefully to their problem. Then he asked them to bring him a large piece of cloth, and he placed the stone in the centre. He asked a man from each tribe to hold a corner of the cloth. Then he told them to carry the stone to the Kaaba. There, he placed the stone carefully into its place with his own hands. Now all of the tribes had shared in the honour of returning the Black Stone to its place.

'You should have seen how the people praised the way that Muhammad* settled that argument!' the doves cooed.

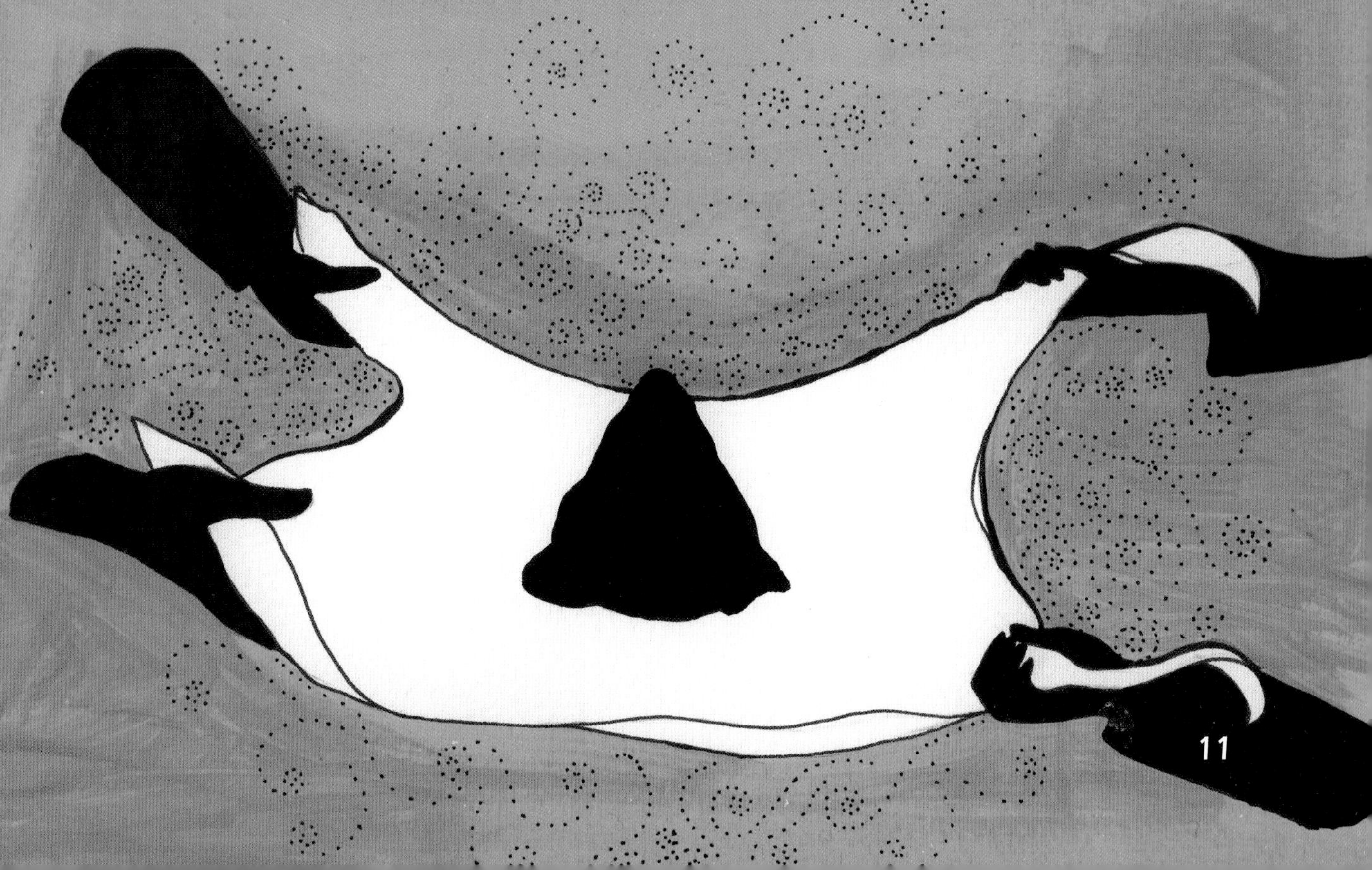

The spider loved to hear these stories, and the doves had many to tell. Muhammad* played with the young and helped the old. He was friendly with both the rich and the poor, and he shared everything he had. Muhammad* was kind to animals and told people not to overburden them. He even trod lightly upon the earth! The spider came to love Muhammad* even though it had never seen him. It recognised him for what he truly was, a Messenger and Prophet of God.

Day followed night and night followed day, and time passed. The doves raised one brood after another and helped them learn to fly, until they could leave and make nests of their own. The spider would tell the chicks stories of Muhammad* and sing them to sleep. It was a very happy little spider.

One day the doves were gone for a very long time. When they finally returned, they had some terrible news. 'Muhammad* is in danger!' they gasped, as they fluttered about fearfully. 'Why, what has happened?' asked the spider in alarm.

'The leaders of Makkah do not like his words,' the doves replied, 'and they do not like that people are following him'. 'Why not?' asked the little spider, in surprise.

'Muhammad* wants to change many things about Makkah. He* says that it is wrong to be cruel, and that the people should treat all living things with kindness. He said that farm and riding animals should not be overworked, but they don't believe in giving *animals* rights. He told the Makkans to share their wealth with the poor and take care of the weak, but the rich people want to keep their money. What made them most angry, however, was his saying that people should stop worshipping idols of wood and stone. He wants them to turn to the One God, Creator of all. So the leaders of Makkah have told him to stop.'

'The leaders tried to bribe him* with riches, power and beauty. They said, "We will make you our king, give you gold and silver, and give you the most beautiful woman to marry. Just stop telling everyone to worship only One God."

'They are afraid that people from other tribes will stop coming to Makkah if their gods and idols are not welcome,' the doves explained. 'But Muhammad* said "Even if you place the sun in my right hand and the moon in my left, I will never give up my sacred duty to call people to God."'

The doves were very frightened. In hushed voices they said, 'Some of the leaders are planning to stop the Prophet once and for all – they want to kill him!'

'Oh, no!' said the little spider, in shock. 'I must do something.' But the spider did not know what it could do. It was such a small creature, and so far away. But destiny can be a strange thing, and the destiny of a spider is no different.

The moon rose above the sand dunes, and on a camel riding towards Mount Thawr was a man who needed the help of a little spider. His name was Muhammad*. The angel Gabriel had warned him of his enemies' plot, and he had escaped the city just in time. With him were his trusted friend Abu Bakr+, and a guide. They all knew that they were being followed by men who wanted to stop Muhammad* and his message.

As the Prophet* and his companions approached Mount Thawr, danger was not far behind. They had to find a hiding place quickly. Muhammad* and Abu Bakr+ got down from their camels. Abu Bakr+ climbed the mountain and entered the cave, looking out for snakes or scorpions. He smiled as he saw the dove's nest, and gently pulled aside a spider's web near the entrance. The cave was barely big enough to hide two people, but it was the best place they could find. It would have to do! Muhammad* and Abu Bakr+ thanked the guide, took their bags of supplies and returned the camels. There was nothing more to do but to wait patiently, and pray.

How furious the leaders of Makkah were when they discovered that Muhammad* had escaped! They hired an expert tracker, a scout with keen eyes, to find and follow his tracks in the desert. They promised a big reward: 'A hundred camels for anyone who finds Muhammad* and Abu Bakr+, dead or alive!' they said.

Back at the cave, the gentle doves watched the Prophet of God* and his friend, but they did not fly away. They knew who this man was. 'How sweet he smells! And how peaceful he looks. Maybe he has crumbs in his pockets,' they thought hopefully. The spider was watching, and it recognized him, too. There was no mistaking him: "A face like the moon and a beaming smile, with a small gap between his front teeth." The spider was overjoyed to see the Prophet* at last! Then its joy turned to fear as it saw that danger was close behind.
'I must help him,' thought the little spider, 'but what can I do? I am so small and weak, and now even my web is broken.'

Then an inspiration from God came to the spider's heart. 'MY WEB! That's it!' thought the spider. 'My silk is my strength and I can spin very fast. God-willing, those foolish men will never guess that the Prophet* is in this cave.'

And that is what it did: it began to spin a web across the mouth of the cave, as quickly as it could. It leapt from stone to stone. Silken lines crossed this way and that, forming a beautiful pattern. Finally when it had finished the spider sat right in the middle of its web, as if to say, 'None shall pass!'

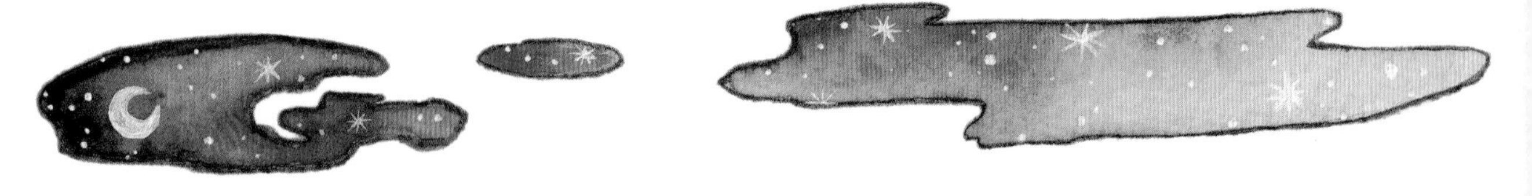

Now the search party from Makkah had been hunting for Muhammad* for some time. They had started their search to the north of the city, in the direction of Yathrib, but found nothing. Then they checked all paths east and west. Still nothing. Finally, tired and hungry, they turned their attention to the south, towards Thawr. There, under layers of sheep tracks, the scout found some recent camel dung. 'This was left by city camels,' he said with confidence. 'The tracks lead up towards that cave.'

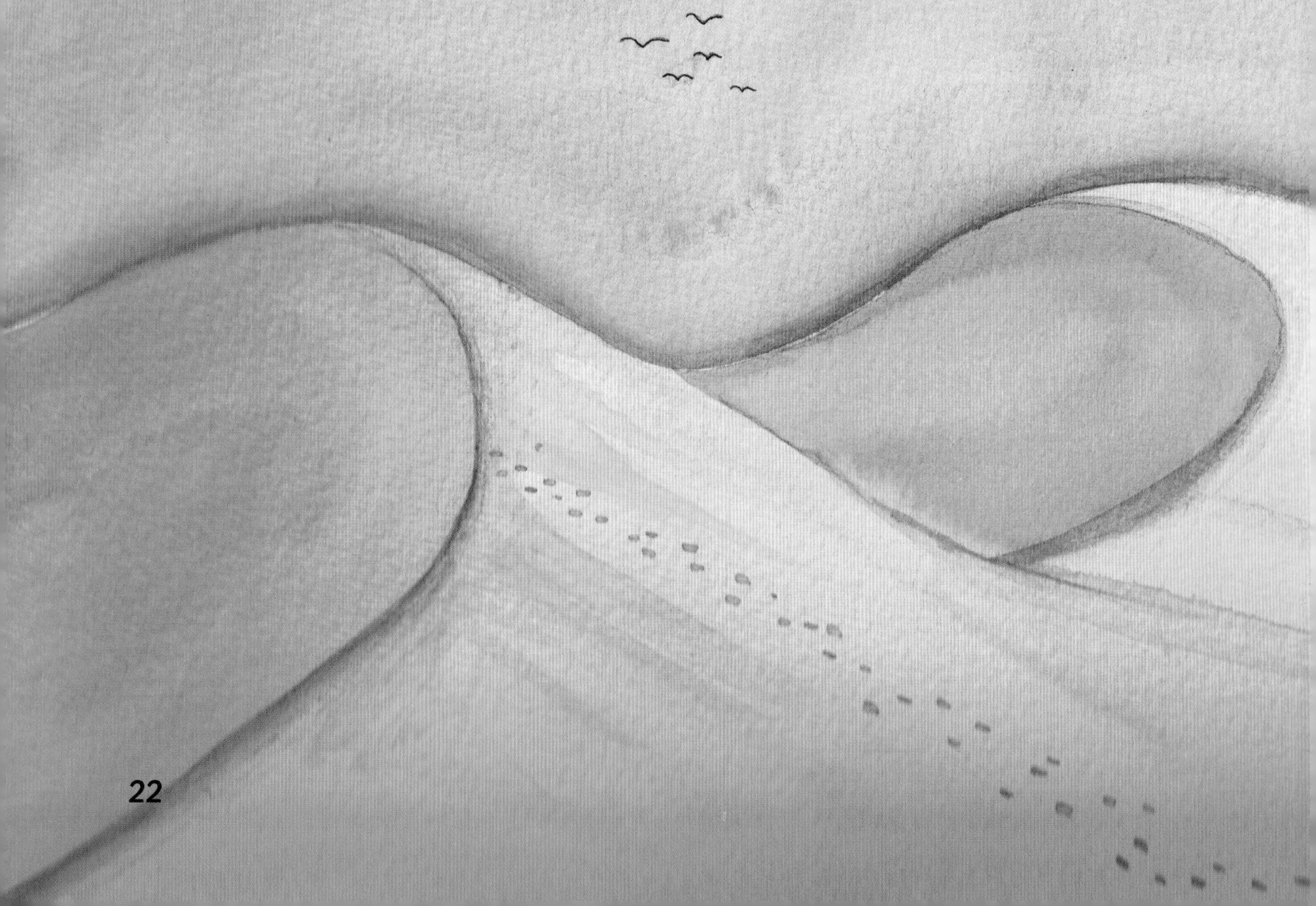

By this time, most of the men were tired and wanted their suppers. Some thought that they were on a wild goose chase. None of them wanted to climb up the rocky, steep mountain face to inspect the cave. 'He's probably long gone by now!' they grumbled.

'No one can be in there!' observed one man. 'See – there are doves nesting up there who have not flown!'

The scout and another man climbed up to get a closer look. 'There is an unbroken web across the mouth of the cave,' the scout sighed in frustration. 'If they were in here, the web would have been broken.'

'Well, I'm sure that city-fed camels passed by here only a short time ago!' the other replied.

Abu Bakr+ stood at the back of the cave, wiped a tear from his eye and raised his hands in prayer as the men argued outside. 'If they only look down at their feet, they will see us!' he whispered very softly.

'Do not fear,' whispered the Prophet*, reassuringly. 'God is with us. How can you worry for two men whose Companion is God Himself?'

'I am only afraid for your sake, O Messenger of God,' replied Abu Bakr+.

And the two men marvelled in silence at the doves that had remained in their nest, and the delicate threads of the spider's lace that had been spun so quickly.

'As we stand here bickering,' one of the men said, 'Muhammad* and Abu Bakr+ are speeding away from us into the desert. Stop wasting time; maybe we can still catch them if we head north again. We must have somehow missed their tracks going towards Yathrib.' At those words, a few of the men mounted their horses and rode away. The others soon followed them.

As the Makkans rode off into the desert, the little spider couldn't believe its eight eyes. Small though it was, it had helped save the beloved Prophet* from harm!

'Thank you, God, for allowing a humble creature like myself to help Your Messenger, the Best of Creation!'

So prayed the spider, one of the smallest of creatures, to God, the Lord of all creation.

After another day in hiding, the two companions left the doves and spider behind in their cave. They carried on with their long journey, hundreds of miles north, through harsh desert to the city of Yathrib!

Now there have been many great journeys– to the icy poles, to the thickest jungles and even to the moon– but this journey changed the world like no other. This was the **Hijra**, the journey that allowed Islam to grow and spread. In Yathrib the Prophet* and Abu Bakr+ received a warm and joyous welcome. Men, women and children sang songs in the Prophet's honour. The people embraced him and his message with open arms, and *their* city became *his* city. Yathrib became known as 'Madinat al-Nabi' – City of the Prophet – or 'Madinah' for short.

From Madinah's fertile soil the new message of peace took root, and Muslims from far and wide left their homes to settle there. Eventually, even the hearts and minds of the Prophet's enemies in Makkah were conquered by goodness, and they joined his growing followers. In those days justice was for all, not just for the rich and powerful. People of different races and tribes, rich and poor, worked together as one; and peace ruled the land as it had always ruled the Prophet's* heart.

The cave on Mount Thawr still exists. And although the spider and doves have long been gone, their memory remains in the hearts of people all over the world. They will always be bound to the life of the Prophet of Islam* by their soothing song and silken threads.